This book was **picked** by

Our story begins
one cold **stormy** night,

A toy was created that
caused quite a **fright**,

He was unceremoniously sent *down* the chute,

REJECTS

His name was **Snot**
he was far from cute.

Sticky, green and all alone, he set

off in hope of finding a home.

But the city can feel like a **frightening** place,

For a lonely little fella,
with a funny little face.

Nowhere felt safe

Until he chanced upon

for the unwanted toy,

somewhere that filled him with joy.

Then the toys looked scared,
though not of Snot.

But the **50** ft monster in the parking lot.

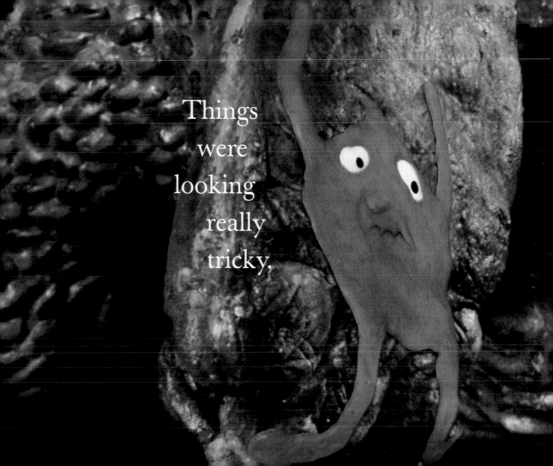

Things
were
looking
really
tricky,

But **Snot** was brave
and **Snot** was sticky,

'Our hero' he heard,
'You saved the day'.

When he saw who had spoken
his knees gave way.

Now here at Smyths Toys Superstores,
he likes it a lot,

The one place where kids are
allowed to pick **Snot**.